American JAZZ

BILLIE HOLIDAY

EARLE RICE JR.

Mitchell Lane
PUBLISHERS
P.O. Box 196
Hockessin, Delaware 19707

American JAZZ

Benny Goodman

Bessie Smith

Billie Holiday

Charlie Parker

Count Basie

Dizzy Gillespie

Louis Armstrong

Miles Davis

Ornette Coleman

Scott Joplin

Copyright © 2013 by Mitchell Lane Publishers

Printing   1   2   3   4   5   6   7   8   9

PUBLISHER'S NOTE: The facts on which this book is based have been thoroughly researched. Documentation of such research can be found on page 44. While every possible effort has been made to ensure accuracy, the publisher will not assume liability for damages caused by inaccuracies in the data, and makes no warranty on the accuracy of the information contained herein.

**Library of Congress
Cataloging-in-Publication Data**

Rice, Earle.
  Billie Holiday / by Earle Rice, Jr.
     p. cm. — (American jazz)
  Includes bibliographical references and index.
  ISBN 978-1-61228-267-1 (library bound)
  1. Holiday, Billie, 1915–1959—Juvenile literature.
  2. Singers—United States—Biography—Juvenile
  literature. I. Title.
  ML3930.H64R53 2013
  782.42165092—dc23
  [B]
                                            2012008590

eBook ISBN: 9781612283432

                                            PLB

PARENTS AND TEACHERS STRONGLY CAUTIONED:
The story of Billie Holiday's life may not be appropriate for young readers.

Contents

Chapter 1

"The Best Jazz Singer Alive"

Carnegie Hall stands two blocks south of New York City's Central Park. It rises in quiet majesty at 881 Seventh Avenue, between West 56th Street and West 57th Street. Its reddish exterior of narrow Roman bricks reflects a sort of Old World charm. Details fashioned in terracotta and brownstone set off its imposing façade. For over a century, an appearance in its Main Hall has marked the high point in the careers of countless performing artists.

A list of performers featured at Carnegie Hall through the years reads like a who's who of music and entertainment immortals. Year after year, the finest musical talents in the business have worked their own special brands of magic on the hall's refined audiences: Benny Goodman, Judy Garland, Count Basie, Bill Haley and His Comets, the Beatles, the Beach Boys, Pink Floyd, Jay-Z, and the list goes on. Among the many magical performances at the hall, one concert by a single female vocalist cries out for special remembrance. It was billed simply as "Lady Sings the Blues."

The *lady* of the title was Billie Holiday, known in the music world as "Lady Day." Her dear friend Lester Young named her so. She called him Prez (or Pres), short for *President of Tenor Saxophonists*. Don Friedman, another friend, booked the concert for November 10, 1956. He scheduled her performance to happen at about the same time as the recent publication of a shortened version of her book of the same name. In the opinion of many critics, the book was totally forgettable; her performance on stage, absolutely memorable.

Billie played to two houses that night: the first show started at eight; the second, at midnight. The first was recorded. A crew of topflight jazz musicians played in a muted, swinging tempo behind her. These jazz greats included Carl Drinkard on piano, joined in the rhythm section by Chico Hamilton (drums), Carson Smith (bass), and Kenny Burrell (guitar). Coleman Hawkins and Roy Eldridge provided the backing horns (saxophone and trumpet, respectively).

Unlike most ordinary concerts, Lady Sings the Blues began with a narration. "The most unusual feature of the presentation," observed John Chilton, one of Billie's biographers, "was that the links between Billie's songs were provided by Gilbert Millstein (a *New York Times* writer) who read four long excerpts from Billie's book."[1] His prose introduction served notice to the audience that the production they were about to witness would be anything but ordinary. "Some of the packed audience fidgeted as Millstein read," Chilton continued, "but most of them tolerated the reading in silence, saving their reactions for Billie's singing."[2] The audience greeted her with hearty applause, and she did not disappoint them.

In her opening selection, Billie voiced the tormented lyrics to "Lady Sings the Blues." She had collaborated on the song with pianist/composer Herbie Nichols. Billie wrote the words; Nichols composed the music. Her hushed rendition of her own sad words revealed the pain of her past loves. She bared herself to the world. The audience felt her pain and took her into their hearts. Billie continued with many of the numbers closely associated with her up-and-down career: "Ain't Nobody's Business If I Do," "God Bless the Child," "Trav'lin' Light," and nineteen others. She closed out an extraordinary performance with her touching and intimate interpretation of George Gershwin's "I Loves You Porgy." The audience punctuated her closing with thunderous applause.

Writer Nat Hentoff, reporting on Billie's performance that evening in the jazz magazine *DownBeat,* wrote: "The audience was hers before she sang, greeting her and saying goodbye with heavy applause, and at one time the musicians too, applauded. It was a night when Billie was on top, the best jazz singer alive."[3] Jazz enthusiasts can hear her Carnegie concert on *The Essential Billie Holiday* (Verve) and judge for themselves.

Billie Holiday traveled to the top of her profession on a highway riddled with potholes. She began her journey in a hospital in Philadelphia, Pennsylvania, on April 7, 1915. Shortly after her birth, she was moved to Baltimore, Maryland, where she grew up as Eleanora Fagan (or Gough). In the oddly unique opening lines of her autobiography *Lady Sings the Blues,* she signaled the start of a life less ordinary. "Mom and Pop were just a couple of kids when they got married," she wrote. "He was eighteen, she was sixteen, and I was three."[4] Actually, Billie's parents never married. And Mom was older than Pop.

Though impossible to know for sure, young Eleanora's father is widely believed to be Clarence Holiday. He eventually became a successful jazz guitarist, playing with the likes of Fletcher Henderson. Eleanora and her teenage mother, Sarah (Sadie) Fagan, saw little of Clarence during Eleanora's early years. Sadie worked a variety of domestic jobs in and out of Baltimore. When working out of town, she sent Eleanora to in-laws in Baltimore to help raise her. In early twentieth-century America, African Americans were still considered lower than second-class citizens. Living did not come easy for them, and this was especially true in Baltimore—a dismal place for most African Americans to live. Sixty years after the Civil War (1861–1865), equality still eluded

Eleanora Fagan, the future Billie Holiday, at the age of two.

them. In the city where the future Billie Holiday grew up, dreams of a better life remained out of the reach of most black citizens.

In 1920, Sadie's marriage to longshoreman Philip Gough brought stability to young Eleanora's life for a while. But less than three years later, Gough abandoned his family. Sadie and Eleanora moved to a dockside area in Baltimore known as Fells Point in 1925. Sadie eventually opened a restaurant, and Eleanora helped out, cooking, waiting on tables, and washing dishes.

Eleanora had just been released from the House of Good Shepherd for Colored Girls, a Catholic school for wayward girls. She had been sent there for skipping school. Some writers suggest that older girls at the school had sexually abused her. Things got even worse for young Eleanora at Fells Point, a red-light district filled with bars and brothels.

Eleanora's work at the restaurant brought her in contact with Baltimore's night people. One madam tipped her for running errands and doing housekeeping chores at her brothel. While working there, Eleanora began singing along to records by Bessie Smith and Louis Armstrong on the madam's Victrola (record player).

One day Eleanora returned home after school to find a neighbor man in her apartment. He lured her to a friend's house and raped her. "I'll never forget that night," Eleanora wrote later. "It's the worst thing that can happen to a woman. And here it was happening to me when I was ten."[5] More bad luck followed: Sadie's business failed. At the end of 1928, Sadie went to find work in New York. She left Eleanora behind again in the care of in-laws.

At age thirteen, Eleanora, mature for her age and already quite glamorous, found work singing in some of the local clubs until Sadie sent for her. She had taken her first steps toward becoming Billie Holiday—"the best jazz singer alive."

House of Good Shepherd

Eleanora Fagan—the girl who was to become Billie Holiday—did not like school very much. While a student at West Baltimore's Public School 104, she began cutting classes at every opportunity. After her stepfather Philip Gough abandoned the family, Eleanora was left alone a lot while her mother worked. She began to develop her own ideas about making her way in life. In 1924, at age nine, Eleanora turned to the street for an education more interesting and exciting than she had found in the classroom. But her truancies soon caught the attention of probation officer Anna M. Dawson.

On January 5, 1925, Eleanora appeared before Juvenile Court. Magistrate T. J. Williams declared her "a minor without proper care and guardianship." He sent her to the city's Catholic-run House of Good Shepherd for Colored Girls at Calverton Road and Franklin Street (pictured) for a year. Upon her arrival at the forbidding red-brick building, the Little Sisters of the Poor gave her the protective name of Madge (later Theresa) to preserve her privacy. Under the disciplined control of the Catholic nuns, Eleanora found the guidance and security that had been missing in her life.

While at the Catholic home for wayward girls, "Madge" resumed her formal education under Sister Margaret Touhe. The two bonded and remained lifelong friends. On a visit to the school in the 1950s, Margaret's former pupil sang for the girls. By then, Eleanora had won fame under her new name of Billie Holiday.

Chapter 2

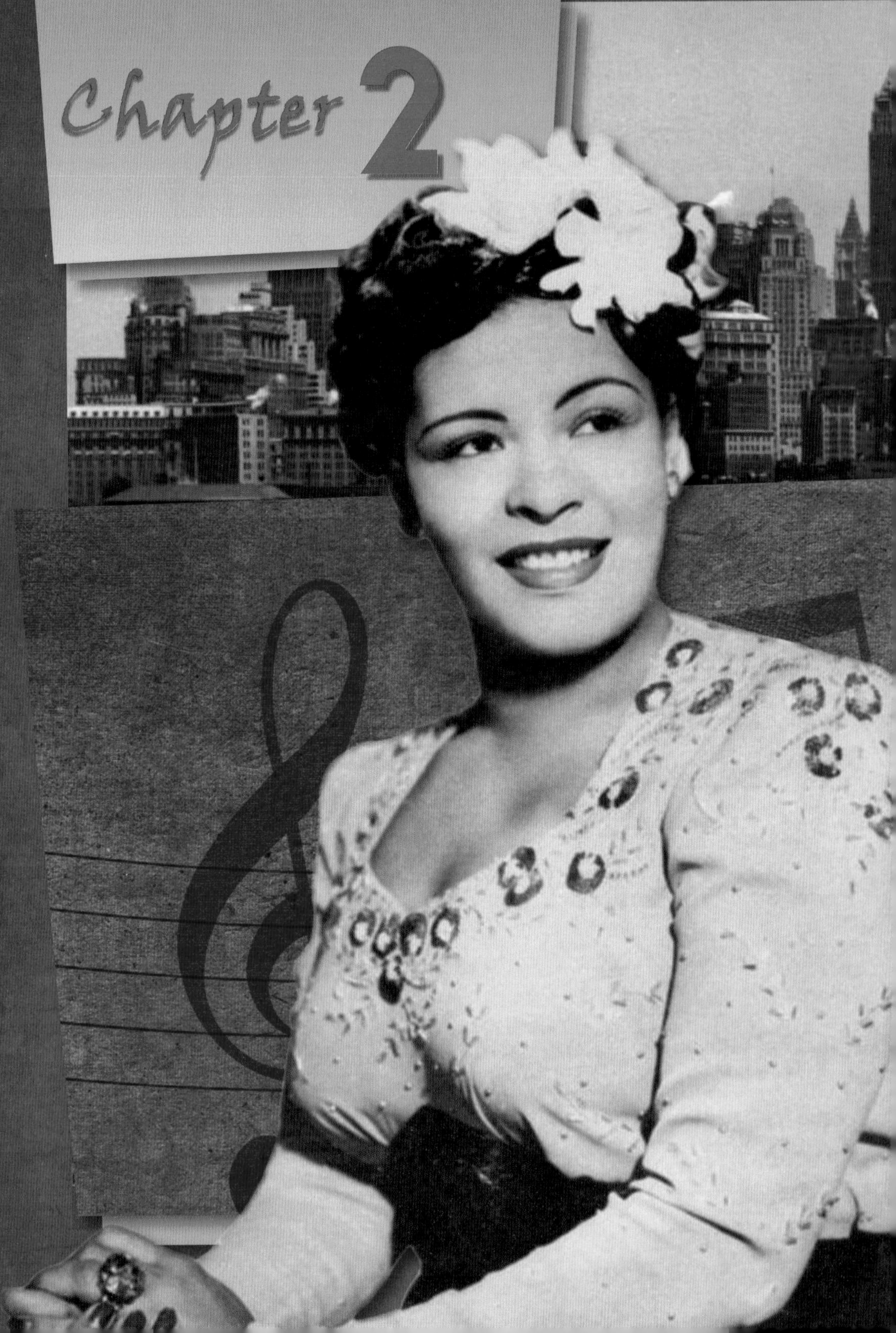

Heartaches and Betrayal

Eleanora left Baltimore for New York in early 1929. As she wrote later, "I was traveling light . . . but I was traveling."[1] When Eleanora arrived in New York, Sadie rented rooms in an apartment house in Harlem. Harlem begins at 110th Street and runs north to 155th Street. It was then undergoing a cultural renewal. Its population had risen from 90,000 in 1910 to almost 325,000 in 1929. By then, an influx of southern blacks had turned it into a mostly African-American community. Sadie and Eleanora lived at 151 West 140th Street. The building belonged to a woman named Florence Williams. She ran one of the biggest brothels in all of Harlem.

Sadie, struggling to survive, had gone to work for Florence. Eleanora, declaring she was twenty-one, soon joined her. As she recalled later, "In a matter of days, I had my chance to become a strictly twenty-dollar call girl—and I took it."[2] In early May, both Sadie and Eleanora got caught up in a police roundup of play-for-pay ladies. Manhattan authorities sentenced Eleanora to 100 days in an island workhouse in the East River. Sadie received a lighter sentence. Mother and daughter reunited in October and moved to a new apartment in Brooklyn.

In her new neighborhood, Eleanora met neighbor Kenneth Hollon, a struggling young saxophone player. They became friends, and she began singing along with him. Their friendship marked the start of her lifelong fascination with the saxophone and those who played it. It also

Billie and her mother, Sarah "Sadie" Fagan Gough, in a nightclub on 52nd Street. Though their relationship knew more than its share of ups and downs, mother and daughter loved each other deeply.

sparked her ambition to make her way through life as a professional singer. Sadie went to work as a domestic, but Eleanora declared she would "never scrub floors or keep house for white folks."[3]

Eleanora Fagan realized that her name did not fit her ambition, so she changed it. Borrowing the first name of the actress Billie Dove, she added her father's surname to it, and Billie Holiday was born. The name—and the unique talent that went with it—would one day take its place among the greatest names in American jazz.

The informal team of Hollon and Holiday began appearing in some of the local clubs. They included the Gray Dawn in Queens, the Brooklyn Elks Lodge, and Pod and Jerry's (The Catagonia Club) on West 133rd Street in Harlem. At the Gray Dawn, Billie sang Fats Waller's "My Fate Is in Your Hands" and "Honeysuckle Rose"; also "How Am I to Know?" by Jack King and Dorothy Parker. Hollon and Holiday ended their arrangement in the spring of 1930. Billie continued on as a single performer.

While appearing at Pod and Jerry's, Billie fell in love with pianist Bobby Henderson. Singer Mae Barnes believed he was "the only man I think she ever loved in her life."[4] But Bobby was a quiet, thoughtful man, ill-suited to Billie's fast lifestyle. She was already into marijuana and was beginning to drink heavily. They worked the bar and grille circuit together for a while, but their engagement ended in December 1934.

At some point in 1932, Billie came in contact with her father. Clarence Holiday was working with Fletcher Henderson's band at the Roseland Ballroom at 52nd Street near Broadway. Some observers saw their relationship as strained; others thought it amicable. Either way, their careers kept them apart most of the time. But Billie loved him deeply.

Bandleader Fletcher Henderson's orchestra was considered by many to be the best-loved band in the black community in 1928. It was known as the best band with the best music. Musicians, including Clarence Holiday, knew if they could make it there, they could make it anywhere.

Billie's individual style caught on quickly with club patrons and fellow musicians alike. She never sang the same song the same way twice. In the view of jazz writer Leonard Feather, "It is impossible to describe Billie's voice: the tart, gritty timbre, the special way of bending a note downward, the capacity for reducing a melody to its bare bones or, when it seemed appropriate, for retaining all its original qualities."[5] Billie made every song in her repertoire sound like a new song every time she sang it.

In early 1933, young socialite and jazz enthusiast John Hammond stopped into Covan's Club Morocco at 148 West 133rd Street. He had intended to hear vocalist Monette Moore. To his surprise, he learned that Billie had replaced Monette. Her sizzling version of "Wouldja for a Big Red Apple?" pleased him no end. "She was not a blues singer, but sang popular songs in a manner that made them completely her own," he wrote later. "She had an uncanny ear, an excellent memory for lyrics, and she sang with an exquisite sense of phrasing. . . . I decided that night that she was the best jazz singer I had ever heard."[6]

Word of a talented new club singer began to circulate around town. Celebrities started dropping in to see and hear her at Pod and Jerry's. Notable personalities such as playwright Charles Laughton, actor Paul Muni, musicians Red Norvo and his wife Mildred Bailey, clarinetist Benny Goodman, and many others became regular patrons. Billie's reputation as a fine new vocalist continued to grow.

Benny Goodman

In November, Hammond arranged for Billie to make her recording debut. He put together a nine-piece studio band led by Benny Goodman. Billie, at age eighteen, recorded two songs for Columbia Records: "Your Mother's Son-in-Law" and "Riffin' the Scotch." (*Riffing* means to toss musical phrases back and forth between the brass and reed sections.) "Riffin' the Scotch" was written especially for Billie. The original words did not work for her, so songwriter Johnny Mercer fine-tuned the lyrics for a better match. Using Louis Armstrong's musical talent for making things up as he went along, and calling on Bessie Smith's simple stylings, Billie added a new and lasting theme to her songbook—the timeless story of a woman unlucky in love. Billie Holiday sang of breaking hearts and cheating men—and out of heartaches and betrayals she fashioned her signature style.

Defining *Jazz*

Jazz is many things to many people. When asked what jazz is, any ten people will likely give ten different answers. And each answer will just as likely be true. The definition of *jazz*—or *jass, jas,* or *jaz*—is as elusive as its origins.

Many believe that the word *jazz*, as it is now spelled, originated out of the West African dialect. It probably did, but a positive connection has never been proven. According to *The Musical Quarterly* (January 1935), "The word jazz in its progress toward respectability has first meant sex, then dancing, then music. It is associated with a state of nervous stimulation."[7]

Technically, *jazz* is defined as music of American origin characterized by improvisation, syncopation, and usually a regular or forceful rhythm. But *Harper's Magazine* (April 1936) contends that jazz defies definition: "Jazz is a style, not a form, and styles can only be described, not defined."[8] However jazz lovers may choose to describe it, jazz—in its developed state—is an original American art form.

American jazz originated in the black communities of the South in the late nineteenth century. Most sources trace the beginnings of its popularity to Storyland, the bawdy red-light district of bars and bordellos in New Orleans. Its unique sound derives from a blend of African  rhythms and Western harmonies. Jazz represents a major black contribution to American culture. Perhaps writer Richard Knight put it best: "It is the nobility of the race put into sound."[9]

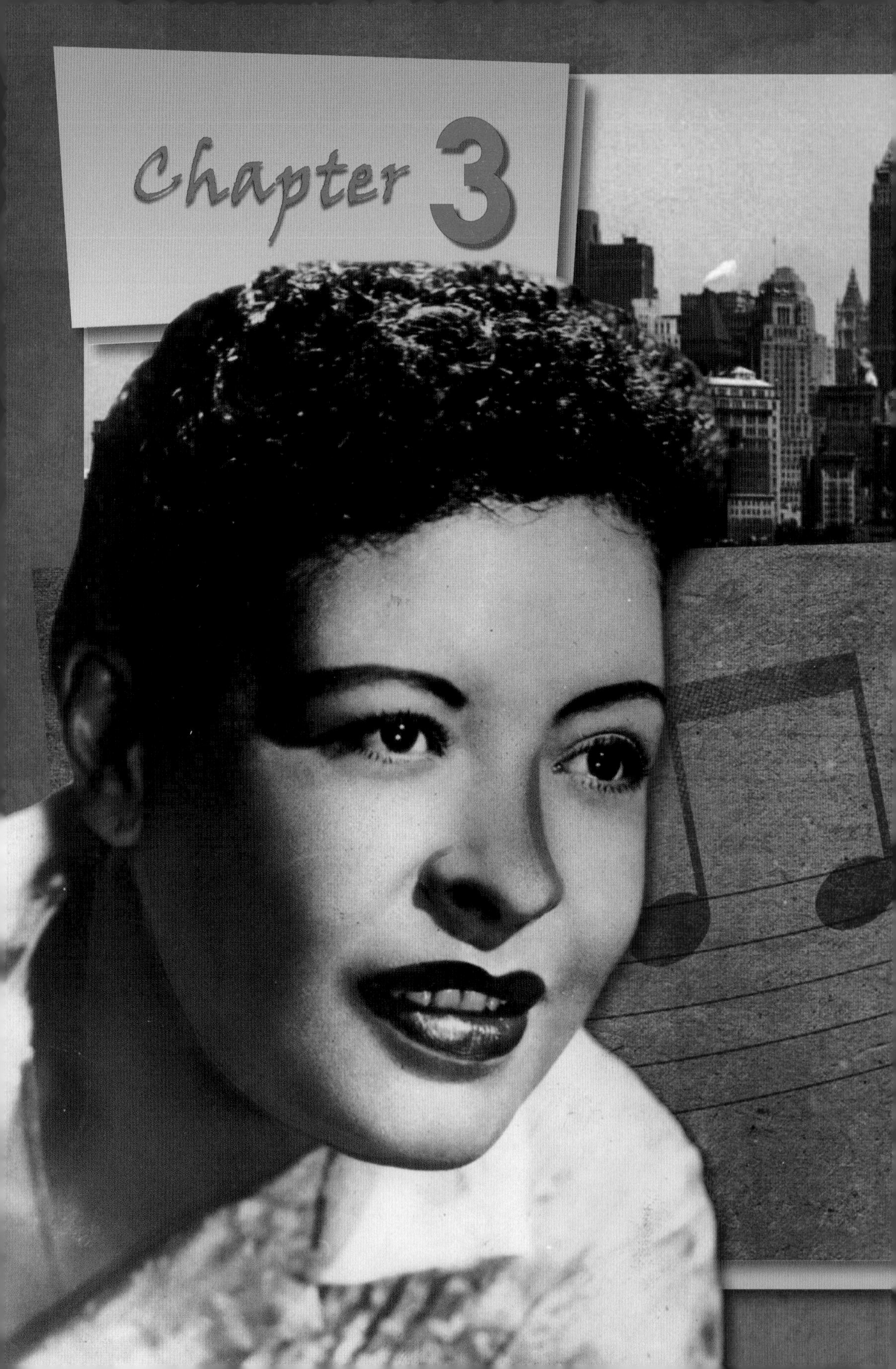
Chapter 3

Billie's Way

Billie's career picked up speed in 1934. In November, she appeared at the Apollo Theater, between 7th and 8th Avenues on the north side of 125th Street. Famous for its Apollo Amateur Nights, the two-balconied theater holds almost two thousand people. Successful performances there have heightened the careers of some of the biggest stars in show business. Lena Horne, Sarah Vaughan, Billy Eckstine, and numerous others owed the Apollo for boosting their careers.

Apollo owner Frank Schiffman booked Billie on the advice of Ralph Cooper, then master of ceremonies at the theater. Cooper had heard her at the Hot-Cha Club and told Schiffman: "You never heard singing so slow, so lazy, with such a drawl . . . it ain't the blues—I don't know what it is, but you got to hear her."[1]

Hear her he did. Billie appeared with Bobby Henderson on piano for the week of November 23. Reports on Billie's Apollo debut vary, but theatrical critics offered faint praise. Nevertheless, Schiffman booked her again in April 1935, this time with Ralph Cooper's band.

Reports of her second gig at the Apollo again varied from source to source. Billie, in her own words, claimed, "The house broke up."[2] According to her, she sang "The Man I Love" as an unplanned encore. She then left the stage quickly with applause resonating in her ears. Schiffman held her over for a second week. "This was one of the few times it happened there," she said, "if I do say so myself. And I damn well do."[3]

In 1935, Billie appeared briefly in Duke Ellington's short film *Symphony in Black, A Rhapsody of Negro Life.* Its arty production, enhanced by Ellington's sparkling compositions, scored big wherever it played. Billie sang a song named "Saddest Tale," adapted to tell of another lost love. Her cameo role was one of the few times she appeared on film. The brief stint increased her exposure on her climb to stardom.

John Hammond brought Billie back to the recording studio in July 1935. As producer, Hammond assembled a seven-piece pickup band for one engagement only. The group featured Teddy Wilson on piano, and

Billie and bandleader-pianist-composer-arranger Edward Kennedy "Duke" Ellington rehearse for his short film *Symphony in Black: A Rhapsody of Negro Life.* The film showcased Billie's rare talent and delicate contralto.

included Benny Goodman on clarinet and Roy Eldridge on trumpet. Billie recorded two songs under the Columbia label: "I Wished on the Moon" and "What a Little Moonlight Can Do."

On the latter title, as described by John Chilton, "she seems out to prove that her talents weren't restricted to slow torch-songs; her great sense of rhythm and versatility are highlighted as she swings her way through an amazingly fast version of the song."[4]

From 1935 to 1939, Billie returned to the recording studio several more times. The recordings she made during this four-year span rank among her very best. Though often called a blues singer, she recorded only two genuine blues pieces in this period: "Billie's Blues" in 1936 and "Long Gone Blues" in 1939.

Much of Billie's portfolio consisted of popular songs by popular songwriters. Her renderings included "The Man I Love," "I Must Have That Man," "I Cried for You," and many more. Billie stayed true to her theme.

In June 1936, a New York talent agent booked Billie into the Grand Terrace Ballroom in Chicago for seventy-five dollars a week. Ed Fox, the dance hall's owner, did not like her style. "Everybody says you sing too slow,"[5] he said. During the argument that ensued, Billie began to hurl furniture at him. He fired her, and she returned to New York without pay. She later told her manager, Joe Glaser: "I want to sing like I want to sing . . . that's my way of doing it."[6] Billie always did things her way.

In January 1937, Billie began the year with another recording session with Benny Goodman, Teddy Wilson, and newcomer Lester Young on the saxophone. In a studio clouded in marijuana smoke, they recorded "He Ain't Got Rhythm," "This Year's Kisses," "Why Was I Born?" and "I Must Have That Man." Remarkably, that waxing went down as one of the greatest recording sessions in the annals of jazz.

The two distinctly different personalities of Holiday and Young clicked right from the start. Billie never sang better; Lester's mellow saxophone anticipated and enhanced her every word and tone. Their interplay of voice and horn marked the start of a personal and professional relationship that would last until Lester's death. Lady Day and the Prez, as they called each other, went together like words and music. They shared an instant connection during Billie's fine treatment of "I Must Have That Man."

Biographer John Chilton later wrote of their oneness that day: "Lester's obbligato [accompanying part] and solo are so close to Billie's mood that one could imagine that the two had worked closely together for years—in fact they had only been introduced a few hours before."[7] Their personal and professional relationship spanned twenty-two years. They became closer than pages in a songbook.

Only a month after finding a musical soul mate in Prez, Billie lost her father. Clarence Holiday died of pneumonia in Dallas on February 23, 1937. He was only thirty-nine. Clarence had sought treatment at several hospitals in Dallas. Because of the racial prejudices existing then, each hospital turned him away. When a veteran's hospital took him in at last, it was too late. A bitter Billie later wrote, "[I]t wasn't the pneumonia that killed him, it was Dallas, Texas."[8] But life and careers must go on.

Billie next toured with William "Count" Basie's band. Basie was known for his recent recording of "One O'Clock Jump." Working with some of the best jazz musicians in the world, Billie developed a poise and vitality that she would seldom show again. Lester Young and trumpet player Buck Clayton complemented her voice and phrasing with superb anticipation. "I would watch her mouth," Clayton noted, "and when I saw that she was going to take a breath or something I knew it was time for me to play between expressions. It's what we call 'filling up the windows.'"[9] Artistically, Billie, Lester, and Buck breathed as one.

Count Basie

After leaving Basie, Billie joined Artie Shaw's orchestra in Boston in 1938. Shaw had already put together a string of popular hits: "Begin the Beguine," "Frenesi," and "Stardust." After his Boston engagement, he and his band headed south. Billie became the first black female singer to tour the segregated South with an integrated band. Shaw saw trouble ahead—and he saw right.

The Prez

Lester Willis Young was born in Woodville, Mississippi, on August 27, 1909. He grew up playing the tenor saxophone in his father's band. He also played clarinet, trumpet, violin, and drums. Lester gained prominence in 1933 as a horn player in Count Basie's orchestra in Kansas City, Missouri.

Known for his smooth musical style and laid-back manner, Lester personified the hipster image of the cool jazzman. His effortless playing style influenced many other tenor saxophonists. His harmonic backings merged seamlessly with Billie Holiday's vocalizings. Together, they awed both musicians and audiences with their artistry. Theirs was an act that few professionals wished to follow.

Unlike Billie, who never learned to read music, Lester arrived at his light, simple style through years of disciplined musical training. Jazz writer and biographer Stuart Nicholson once compared his style with Billie's: "Musically, he had much in common with Billie; he spurned the superfluous, using one well-chosen note in place of many, he loved to syncopate notes temptingly behind the groundbeat, he preferred medium and slow tempos, and, just like Billie, loved marijuana."[10] Unhappily, marijuana, alcohol, and drugs silenced their music before its time.

By all accounts, Lady Day and the Prez were great friends but never dated. Rather, it might be said, they struck a perfect chord together—at least for a little while.

Chapter 4

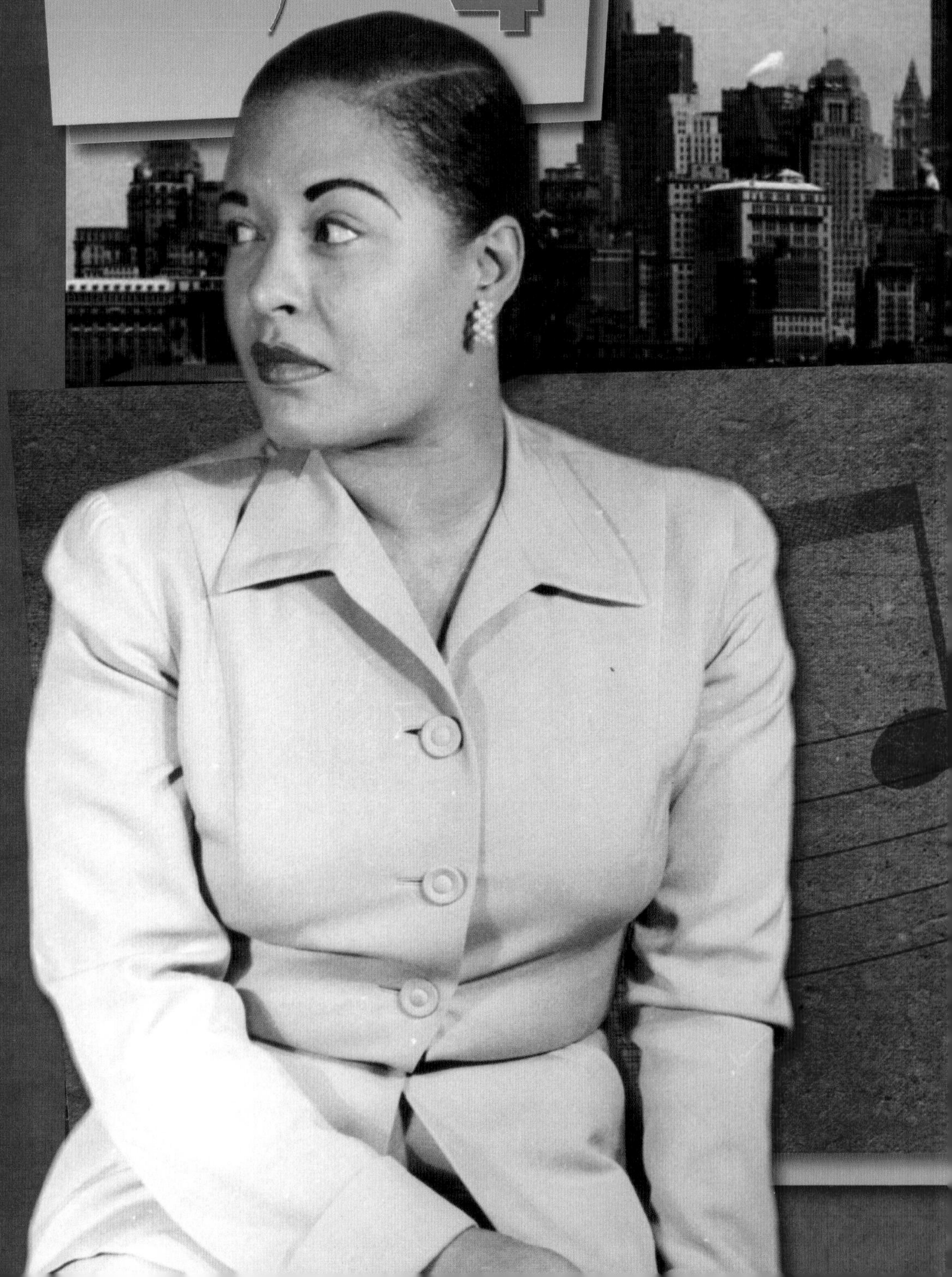

"World on a String"

Artie Shaw knew Billie's presence would pose some problems on a tour of the South. "Billie was a pretty hot-tempered woman," he recalled later. "I could see trouble brewing when we went below the Mason-Dixon line and we took her down there, I don't want to repeat the language, but it was rough stuff."[1]

Billie endured more than her share of hostile treatment and racial slurs in the South. Finding a hotel or a restaurant that would accommodate a black woman was a daily challenge. Billie was often forced to eat in restaurant kitchens. "Some places they wouldn't even let me eat in the kitchen," she recalled. "I got tired of having a federal case over breakfast, lunch, and dinner."[2]

Similar racial indignities continued in the North. In October 1938, Shaw and his orchestra began a residency in the Hotel Lincoln in New York. Billie was not allowed to visit the bar or dining room as were the other band members. She told a reporter for the *New York Amsterdam News*: "Not only was I made to enter and leave the hotel through the kitchen but had to remain alone in a little dark room all evening until I was called on to do my numbers."[3] As time went on, calls for her numbers grew fewer and fewer. Billie left the Artie Shaw Orchestra in December.

Billie's fortune took a turn for the better in January 1939. She opened as the star attraction at Café Society, a newly opened club in New York's Greenwich Village. John Hammond organized the entertainment for club owner Barney Josephson. Billie shared the bandstand with the Frankie Newton Band. Bassist John Williams remembered Billie with fondness. "She had the 'World on a String,' being beautiful, having a hell of a figure, personality plus, and a style of her own that no one could steal."[4]

At Café Society, Billie enjoyed enormous popularity. She was now able to choose her own songs and approve their arrangements. With greater control over her material, her style matured—more polished and enriched with expressive shadings. Though well known in Harlem, Billie remained almost unknown elsewhere at that time. That was about to change. "I opened Café Society as an unknown," she noted later; "I left two years later as a star."[5] Her long booking there ushered in her golden years.

In the America of the 1930s, its citizens still bore the shame of extreme racial intolerance. Lynchings and other violent acts against African Americans still occurred in the South and elsewhere in the United States. The violence disturbed a little-known schoolteacher and poet in New York City. His name was Abel Meeropol. Writing under the pen name of Lewis Allan, he published a protest poem titled "Bitter Fruit." Meeropol later set the poem to music and retitled it "Strange Fruit." The title formed a metaphor for black bodies hanging from southern trees.

Early in 1939, Meeropol presented the song to Café Society owner Barney Josephson, which was just opening in New York. Josephson recalled that "one of the first numbers we put on was called 'Strange Fruit Grows on Southern Trees,' the tragic story of lynching. Imagine putting that on in a night club."[6] He presented the song to Billie.

Billie introduced two songs at Café Society that added a glint of gold to her repertoire: "God Bless the Child," a song she wrote with Arthur Herzog Jr.; and Lewis Allan's "Strange Fruit."

Before Billie began to sing, the club's waiters silenced the clientèle. "The scene was set; house lights went down and only a pin-spot picked out the singer's face," wrote Stuart Nicholson. "On the final chord the lights went out. When the house lights went back up she was gone.

Josephson insisted on no encore to underline the stark imagery of both song and singer."[7] Perhaps no song is more closely associated with Billie Holiday than "Strange Fruit."

"When she was in the spotlight she was absolutely regal," recalled record producer Milt Gabler, "the way she held her head up high, the way she phrased each word and got to the heart of the story in each song."[8] She recorded many songs for Gabler on Commodore Records. They included "Strange Fruit," "Yesterdays," "I Got a Right to Sing the

In April 1939, Billie Holiday sang "Strange Fruit" in a recording session at Brunswick's World Broadcasting Studios. Her backing included (from left to right) bassist John Williams, trumpeter Frankie Newton, and saxophonists Stan Payne and Kenneth Hollon.

Billie performing at Chicago's Offbeat Club in 1939, wearing a gardenia. Gardenias became her visual signature and formed a subtle part of her personality.

Blues," and "Fine and Mellow." Over the span of her career, she also recorded for Decca, Columbia, and Verve.

Inevitably, Billie's lifestyle led her to become involved in numerous relationships over the years. None had led to marriage, including a yearlong affair with pianist Sonny White at Café Society. In January 1940, however, Billie met James Monroe at a friend's birthday party in New York. Monroe was the brother of Clark Monroe, the owner of Monroe's Uptown House where Billie sometimes sang. Jimmy was known as a "sportsman"—a polite name for a hustler. Sadie did not like Jimmy, and mother and daughter often fought over his coming to the house. Nevertheless, Billie married Jimmy on August 25, 1941.

The newlyweds honeymooned in Chicago and moved on to Los Angeles. Billie appeared for the first time on the West Coast at a new club in Los Angeles called The Café Society. (It was not connected with Josephson's Café Society in New York City.) A one-month booking ended when the club closed after two weeks. Billie returned to New York. Jimmy stayed on the West Coast, supposedly to follow up on business opportunities.

In mid-May 1942, Billie learned that Jimmy had been busted for drug smuggling. Her efforts to help him failed, and Jimmy was sentenced to a year in jail. While he did his time, Billie sustained herself with short engagements in Los Angeles, Chicago, and New York. Singing the same songs night after night, her delivery became more predictable and less individually stylized. Her gestures lacked their usual expressiveness. Critics started to wonder whether she had already passed her prime at the age of twenty-seven.

Billie's marriage to Jimmy Monroe was mostly a marriage in name only. It lasted for almost fifteen years, but Jimmy's unfaithful behavior foretold its ending early on. One night he came home with lipstick on his collar. When he tried to explain, Billie told him: "Take a bath, man, don't explain."[9] His infidelity inspired her to write "Don't Explain" with Arthur Herzog. She added it to her compilation of sad songs. "This is one song I couldn't sing without feeling every minute of it,"[10] she said.

Billie jiving to "Fine and Mellow" during a jam session. Though not a blues singer, as such, her intimate style of singing evoked a bluesy mood and led to her often being mislabeled as a blues singer.

At some point early in their marriage, Billie began to experiment with opium and heroin. Friends blamed Jimmy for introducing her to the hard drugs. Billie denied it. "Jimmy was no more the cause of my doing what I did than my mother was,"[11] she wrote.

It really did not matter what hooked her on the hard stuff. Her inevitable addiction to the drugs started her career on a downward spiral. Over the next decade, Billie Holiday went from having the "world on a string" to hanging on by a thread.

Barney's Dream

Barney Josephson had a dream. "I wanted a club where blacks and whites worked together behind the footlights and sat together out front," he once said. "There wasn't, so far as I know, a place like it in New York or in the whole country."[12] In 1938, his dream became a reality when he opened Café Society in a basement room in New York's Sheridan Square.

Two years later, Josephson opened Café Society Uptown on East 58th Street. His legendary supper clubs broke the existing color barrier and allowed blacks and whites to mix in the audience.

Josephson, a former shoe manufacturer, knew little about the jazz and entertainment worlds, so he turned to John Hammond for help. Hammond, Billie Holiday's discoverer, was a shrewd judge of talent. The unlikely pair hit it off at once, and Hammond agreed to handle all the bookings for the two clubs.

Operating under the motto "The Right Place for the Wrong People," Café Society and Café Society Uptown featured a near-endless array of musicians, dancers, and other performers bound for greatness. The list of future stars included such talents as Billie Holiday, Lena Horne, Sarah Vaughan, Hazel Scott, Mary Lou Williams, Art Tatum, Teddy Wilson, Eddie Heywood, and many more. Despite the success of Josephson's clubs, he later remarked, "I still think I know more about shoes than I do about the café business."[13] Holiday, Horne, Vaughan, and a host of others might disagree.

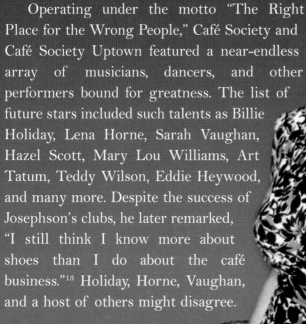

Chapter 5

Lady in Satin

America was at war during the first half of the 1940s. People grew preoccupied with events in Europe and the South Pacific. The nation's musical tastes began to shift to popular songs with the advent of such singers as Frank Sinatra, Perry Como, and others. Yet each generation owes something to its predecessor. "Lady Day," Sinatra said in 1958, "is unquestionably the most important influence on American popular singing in the last 20 years."[1]

In 1943, after Jimmy Monroe was released from prison, he went to work at an aircraft factory in California. Billie continued to work the club circuit in New York, appearing at Kelly's Stables, the Onyx Club, and the Yacht Club. Her recording contract with Columbia had expired, but she signed with Decca Records in 1944. Of her Decca recordings, "Lover Man" stood out as her most popular and enduring offering.

By 1944, Billie had crossed the line from the heavy use of alcohol and marijuana into the volatile world of opium and heroin addiction. Even so, she continued to give some of her finest performances at small clubs on 52nd Street. She often appeared in jam sessions with the likes of trumpeter Dizzy Gillespie and saxophonists John Coltrane and Charlie Parker. But her addiction was becoming harder to hide.

In December, Billie received word that Jimmy Monroe had been arrested again on drug charges. This time she did not try to help him. She had taken up with a young trumpeter named Joe Guy. "He was a personable cat, nice-looking," guitarist Al Casey recalled. "She was in love with him, I guess. She got around, though."[2] Billie went on the road with Guy and his band.

In October 1945, Billie and Guy had just returned to their hotel after a show in Baltimore. Billie said that suddenly she "felt my mother come up behind me and put her hand on my shoulder."[3] News came of Sadie's death the next day. It crushed Billie. She told Guy, "[Y]ou better be good to me because you're all I've got now."[4] Guy kept Billie supplied with drugs until they split in 1947.

Billie debuted in her first solo concert at New York's Town Hall in February 1946. She followed up as one of the guest stars in Norman Granz's *Jazz at the Philharmonic* at Carnegie Hall in April. With Lester Young on tenor saxophone, she sang "Billie's Blues," "All of Me," "Them There Eyes," and "He's Funny That Way."

Hollywood beckoned to Billie in September. Back on the West Coast, she made her only major film appearance in *New Orleans.* Louis Armstrong played a butler; Billie, a maid. Her role greatly disappointed

Billie at Carnegie Hall

Billie. "I'd fought my whole life to keep from being somebody's damn maid," she said.[5] After attending the premiere of the film with Armstrong, Billie tried to confront her drug demons.

In March 1947, Billie checked into a private hospital in Westchester, New York. But as soon as withdrawal symptoms began, she checked out. With Joe Guy still supplying drugs, Billie could not stay away from them. In May, federal agents arrested Billie and Joe Guy for violating the Narcotics Act in Philadelphia. Billie was convicted and sentenced to one year in the federal reformatory in Alderson, West Virginia. Joe Guy escaped conviction on Billie's self-sacrificing testimony.

Louis Armstrong and Billie Holiday appeared together in the Hollywood musical *New Orleans.* Billie sang "Farewell to Storyville," "The Blues Are Brewin'," and the pop song "Do You Know What It Means to Miss New Orleans."

Billie poses with her boxer, Mister, in the dressing room of New York City's Downbeat Club on 52nd Street.

Billie with her second husband, Louis McKay

Billie gave a farewell concert at Carnegie Hall before reporting to authorities. "She sang 'I'll Be Seeing You,' " wrote Leonard Feather, "and if there were any dry eyes in the house, I failed to observe them."[6] Billie served about ten months and was released on parole on March 16, 1948.

Promoter Ernie Anderson booked her into a Carnegie Hall comeback performance March 27. She opened with "I Cover the Waterfront." A fan had sent her gardenias backstage between sets. She pinned one in her hair. "My old trademark—someone had remembered,"[7] she wrote later. Billie sang thirty songs. Her voice was clear and steady. Critic Jack Egan of *DownBeat* magazine wrote: "Lady Day is back, bigger than ever."[8] But her drug demons remained unconquered.

In 1949, Billie was arrested and tried a second time for drug possession. This time she evaded conviction, but state authorities revoked her cabaret license. She could no longer appear in New York establishments that served liquor. As work became harder to find, she booked short engagements from one end of the country to the other—anything to feed herself and her drug habit.

Billie signed a recording contract with jazz promoter Norman Granz in 1952. She released an album titled *Billie Holiday Sings* that December. The next year, she appeared in a television show called "The Comeback Story." Billie told her story and sang "God Bless the Child." Later that year, she appeared with Duke Ellington at Carnegie Hall. At year's end, Billie left for a long-awaited tour of Europe.

British jazz writer Max Jones noted: "She enjoyed the acclaim she received in Europe—later she said the crowd of 6,000 at London's Albert Hall gave her one or the greatest receptions of her life—and she worked as hard as her health would allow to earn it."[9] But drugs and alcohol had taken a heavy toll on her health.

In 1956, Billie divorced Jimmy Monroe, and on March 28, 1957, she married club manager Louis McKay. McKay became her business manager and tried to break her drug habit. He did not succeed. Billie kept making the rounds of the club circuit, as her voice, career, and health continued to spiral downward.

Billie Holiday where she loved to be—in the bright white arc of the spotlight.

In February 1958, Billie recorded an album called *Lady in Satin.* Her song selection told the story of her life: "You've Changed," "End of a Love Affair," and "Glad to Be Unhappy." Her once clear and steady voice had become a low, gravelly promise of an end in sight. Little more than a year later, in March 1959, Billie's lifelong friend Lester Young—the Prez—died of heart failure hastened by alcoholism. His inimitable Lady Day would join him in death only four months later, at the age of forty-four.

Billie Holiday gave her final performance at the Phoenix Theatre in Greenwich Village on May 25, 1959. Her drug-wracked body had wasted away to a wisp of its former self. Six days later, she collapsed in her apartment and was rushed to the hospital. Despite her critical condition, indignities continued to plague her. While at the Metropolitan Hospital for heart and liver problems, authorities again arrested her for drug possession. They kept guard outside her hospital door until just a few hours before she died on July 17, 1959. The cause was alcohol- and drug-related.

More than 3,000 people attended her funeral services in St. Paul the Apostle Roman Catholic Church on July 21, 1959. Included among her solemn devotees were such greats of the jazz world as Benny Goodman, Gene Krupa, Teddy Wilson, John Hammond, and many other musicians she knew. She was laid to rest with her mother at St. Raymond's Cemetery in the Bronx, New York. She left behind an amazing legacy.

Biographer Colin Larkin, a witness to her contributions: "In defiance of her limited vocal range, Billie Holiday's use of tonal variation and vibrato, her skill at jazz phrasing, and her unique approach to the lyrics of popular songs, were but some of the elements in the work of a truly original artist. . . . Holiday paid her dues in a demanding milieu."[10] For these things and more, Billie Holiday remains an unforgettable jazz icon.

Perhaps no one summed up her life better than her friend Barney Josephson. "There was no other person on the face of this earth who was like her," he said. "Billie Holiday was a single edition."[11]

"Fine and Mellow"

News of Lester Young's death hit Billie Holiday hard. Lady and Prez had drifted apart over the years. No one quite knows why. After attending Lester's funeral services, Billie turned to her escort, jazz writer Leonard Feather, and predicted, "I'll be the next one to go."[12] While in mourning, perhaps Billie's thoughts returned to a day in December 1957 when she last performed with Lester.

Lady and Prez and an all-star group of jazz players had gathered in New York to tape a television show titled *The Sound of Jazz*. Billie sang "Fine and Mellow," a blues song she had written herself. Lester, now sick and weak from alcoholism, stood up long enough for a brief solo. Jazz writer Nat Hentoff described the session eloquently:

COMPLETE BILLIE HOLIDAY LESTER YOUNG
BY ALAIN GERBER-CHRISTIAN BONNET

1

INTEGRALE BILLIE HOLIDAY LESTER YOUNG 1937-1946

[H]e blew the purest, sparest blues chorus I had ever heard. Billie, smiling, nodding to the beat, looked into Prez's eyes, and he into hers. She was looking back, with the gentlest of regrets, at their past. Prez was remembering too. Whatever had blighted their relationship was forgotten in the communion of their music. Sitting in the control room, I felt tears, and saw tears on the faces of most of the others there. The rest of the program was all right, but this had been its climax—the empirical soul of jazz.[13]

Little more than a year and a half later, the music stopped for both Lady and the Prez, but their musical legacy lingers on. Many would call it . . . fine and mellow.

1915 Eleanora Fagan is born on April 7 in Philadelphia, Pennsylvania.

1920 Sarah Fagan (Eleanora's mother) marries Philip Gough; he leaves less than three years later.

1925 After repeatedly skipping school, Eleanora is sent to the House of Good Shepherd for Colored Girls, a Catholic school for wayward girls and young women. In October, she and her mother move to Fells Point, a neighborhood in Baltimore, Maryland.

1929 Eleanora joins her mother in Harlem, New York City; they are arrested for working as call girls. Mother and daughter move to Brooklyn, New York, where Eleanora, who now calls herself Billie Holiday, meets saxophone player Kenneth Hollon.

1934 Billie Holiday and pianist Bobby Henderson are engaged briefly. She appears at the Apollo in November.

1935 Holiday again at the Apollo, and in Duke Ellington's *Symphony in Black, A Rhapsody of Negro Life.*

1937 Clarence Holiday, Billie's reputed father, dies. Billie tours with Count Basie.

1938 She joins the Artie Shaw Orchestra.

1939 Holiday is the star attraction at Café Society in Greenwich Village, where she sings Lewis Allan's "Strange Fruit."

1941 Holiday marries trombonist Jimmy Monroe on August 25.

1942 Jimmy Monroe is arrested on drug smuggling charges.

1943 Holiday appears at Kelly's Stables, the Onyx Club, and the Yacht Club in New York.

1944 Holiday signs with Decca Records.

1946 Holiday debuts in her first solo concert at New York's Town Hall in February, then guest stars in Norman Granz's *Jazz at the Philharmonic* at Carnegie Hall in April.

1947 Holiday enters rehab but does not stay; she and Joe Guy are arrested for narcotics; Holiday is sentenced to one year in prison.

1948 Holiday plays her comeback performance at Carnegie Hall on March 27.

1949 Holiday is arrested again for drug possession but is not convicted.

1952 She appears with Duke Ellington at Carnegie Hall. At the end of the year, Holiday begins a tour of Europe.

1956 Holiday performs two concerts before packed audiences at Carnegie Hall on November 10.

1957 After divorcing Jimmy Monroe, Holiday marries club manager Louis McKay.

1958 Holiday records an album called *Lady in Satin.* Her song selection tells the story of her life.

1959 Her friend Lester "the Prez" Young dies in March. Billie Holiday dies on July 17.

The Quintessential Billie Holiday,
   Vols, 1–9 (Columbia, 1933–1942)
Lady Day: The Complete Billie Holiday on
   Columbia (1933–1944)
The Complete Commodore Recordings
   (1939–1944)
The Commodore Master Takes
   (1939–1944)
Billie Holiday: The Complete Decca
   Recordings (1944–1950)
The Complete Billie Holiday on Verve
   (1945–1959)
Lady in Autumn: The Best of the Verve
   Years (1946–1959)
Lady Sings the Blues (Verve, 1954–1956)
Lady in Satin (Columbia, 1958)
Love Song—Billie Holiday (Columbia,
   1996)
Lady Day: The Best of Billie Holiday
   (Columbia, 2001)
The Ultimate Collection—Billie Holiday
   (Decca, 2005)

Chapter 1 "The Best Jazz Singer Alive"

1. John Chilton, *Billie's Blues: The Story of Billie Holiday, 1933–1959* (New York: Day Books, 1978), p. 171.
2. Ibid.
3. Ken Vail, *Lady Day's Diary* (Chessington, Surrey UK: Castle Communications, 1996), p. 181.
4. Billie Holiday, with William Dufty, *Lady Sings the Blues* (New York: Penguin Books, 1984), p. 5.
5. Ibid., p. 16.

Chapter 2 Heartaches and Betrayals

1. Billie Holiday, with William Dufty, *Lady Sings the Blues* (New York: Penguin Books, 1984), p. 20.
2. Ibid., p. 23.
3. Stuart Nicholson, *Billie Holiday* (Boston: Northeastern University Press, 1995), p. 33.
4. Donald Clarke, *Wishing on the Moon: The Life and Times of Billie Holiday* (New York: Viking, 1994), p. 51.
5. Leonard Feather, "Lady Day," in *Billie Holiday Companion: Seven Decades of Commentary*, edited by Leslie Gourse (New York: Schirmer Books, 1997), p. 10.
6. Donald Clarke, *Billie Holiday: Wishing on the Moon* (Cambridge, MA: Da Capo, 2000), p. 69.
7. Robert S. Gold, *A Jazz Lexicon* (New York: Alfred A. Knopf, 1964), p. 163.
8. Ibid.
9. Wynton Marsalis, "Why We Must Preserve Our Black Heritage," *Ebony,* February 1986, reprinted in November 1990 issue, p. 159.

Chapter 3 Billie's Way

1. John Chilton, *Billie's Blues: The Story of Billie Holiday, 1933–1959* (New York: Day Books, 1978), p. 16.
2. Ibid., p. 17.
3. Billie Holiday, with William Dufty, *Lady Sings the Blues* (New York: Penguin Books, 1984), p. 40.
4. Chilton, p. 24.
5. Stuart Nicholson, *Billie Holiday* (Boston: Northeastern University Press, 1995), p. 76.
6. Chilton, p. 37.
7. Ibid., p. 42.
8. Holiday, p. 68.
9. Donald Clarke, *Billie Holiday: Wishing on the Moon* (Cambridge, MA: Da Capo, 2000), p. 132.
10. Nicholson, p. 52.

Chapter 4 "World on a String"

1. Stuart Nicholson, *Billie Holiday* (Boston: Northeastern University Press, 1995), p. 103.

2. Billie Holiday, with William Dufty, *Lady Sings the Blues* (New York: Penguin Books, 1984), p. 75.
3. Ken Vail, *Lady Day's Diary* (Chessington, Surrey, UK: Castle Communications, 1996), p. 26.
4. John Chilton, *Billie's Blues: The Story of Billie Holiday, 1933–1959* (New York: Day Books, 1978), p. 65.
5. Holiday, p. 92.
6. David Margolick, "Strange Fruit," *Vanity Fair,* September 1998, http://www.ladyday.net/stuf/vfsept98.html
7. Nicholson, p. 113.
8. Ibid., p. 125.
9. Holiday, p. 105.
10. Ibid.
11. Chilton, p. 86.
12. John S. Wilson, "Obituaries: Barney Josephson, Owner of Café Society Jazz Club, Is Dead at 86," *The New York Times,* September 30, 1988, p. 1; http://www.nytimes.com/1988/09/30/obituaries/barney-josephson-owner-of-café-society-jazz-club-is-dead-at-86.html?pagewanted=all&src=pm
13. Ibid.

Chapter 5 Lady in Satin

1. John Chilton, *Billie's Blues: The Story of Billie Holiday, 1933–1959* (New York: Day Books, 1978), p. 92.
2. Stuart Nicholson, *Billie Holiday* (Boston: Northeastern University Press, 1995), p. 142.
3. Billie Holiday, with William Dufty, *Lady Sings the Blues* (New York: Penguin Books, 1984), p. 109.
4. Ibid.
5. Ibid., p. 119.
6. Leonard Feather, *Billie Holiday Anthology: Lady Day Had a Right to Sing the Blues* (Ventura, CA: Creative Concepts Publishing, 2000), p. 5.
7. Holiday, p. 145.
8. Ken Vail, *Lady Day's Diary* (Chessington, Surrey, UK: Castle Communications, 1996), p. 104.
9. Max Jones, "Billie Holiday in England: 1953," in *Billie Holiday Companion: Seven Decades of Commentary,* edited by Leslie Gourse (New York: Schirmer Books, 1997), p. 47.
10. Colin Larkin, "Billie Holiday Biography," Oldies.com, http://www.oldies.com/artist-biography/Billie-Holiday.html, p. 3.
11. Vail, p. 33.
12. Leonard Feather, "Lady Day," in *Billie Holiday Companion: Seven Decades of Commentary,* edited by Leslie Gourse (New York: Schirmer Books, 1997), p. 16.
13. Nat Hentoff, "The Real Lady Day," in *Billie Holiday Companion: Seven Decades of Commentary,* edited by Leslie Gourse (New York: Schirmer Books, 1997), p. 154.

BOOKS

Cole, Forrest. *Billie Holiday*. New York: Infobase Publishing/Chelsea House, 2010.

Ferguson. *Careers in Focus: Music*. Second Edition. New York: Infobase Publishing/Ferguson, 2009.

Fishkin, Rebecca Love. *Singing: A Practical Guide to Pursuing the Art*. Mankato, MN: Compass Point Books, 2010.

Frederick, Sara Gilbert. *Play It Loud! The Rebellious History of Music*. Mankato, MN: Compass Point Books, 2010.

Greene, Meg. *Billie Holiday: A Biography*. Greenwood Biographies. Westport, CT: Greenwood Press, 2007.

WORKS CONSULTED

Chilton, John. *Billie's Blues: The Story of Billie Holiday, 1933–1959*. New York: Day Books, 1978.

Clarke, Donald. *Billie Holiday: Wishing on the Moon*. Cambridge, MA: Da Capo, 2000.

Feather, Leonard. *Billie Holiday Anthology: Lady Day Had a Right to Sing the Blues*. Ventura, CA: Creative Concepts Publishing, 2000.

Gold, Robert S. *A Jazz Lexicon*. New York: Alfred A. Knopf, 1964.

Gourse, Leslie, ed. *Billie Holiday Companion: Seven Decades of Commentary*. New York: Schirmer Books, 1997.

Holiday, Billie, with William Dufty. *Lady Sings the Blues*. New York: Penguin Books, 1984.

Margolick, David. *Strange Fruit: Billie Holiday, Café Society, and an Early Cry for Civil Rights*. Philadelphia, PA: Running Press, 2000.

Nicholson, Stuart. *Billie Holiday*. Boston: Northeastern University Press, 1995.

O'Meally, Robert G. *Lady Day: The Many Faces of Billie Holiday*. New York: Arcade Publishing, 1991.

Vail, Ken. *Lady Day's Diary*. Chessington, Surrey, UK: Castle Communications, 1996.

Weatherford, Carole. *Becoming Billie Holiday*. Honesdale, PA: Wordsong, 2008.

Wilson, John S. "Obituaries: Barney Josephson, Owner of Café Society Jazz Club, Is Dead at 86," *The New York Times,* September 30, 1988, http://www.nytimes.com/1988/09/30/obituaries/barney-josephson-owner-of-café-society-jazz-club-is-dead-at-86.html?pagewanted=all&src=pm

ON THE INTERNET

Billie Holiday: The Official Site of Lady Day
    http://www.billieholiday.com/
Biography.com: "Billie Holiday"
    http://www.biography.com/people/billie-holiday-9341902
Gale Biographies: "Billie Holiday," http://www.gale.cengage.com/free_resources/bhm/bio/holiday_b.htm
Larkin, Colin. "Billie Holiday Biography"
    http://www.oldies.com/artist-biography/Billie-Holiday.html
Nicholson, Stuart. The Dozens: Twelve Essential Billie Holiday Performances, http://www.jazz.com/dozens/b-holiday-dozens

BILLIE HOLIDAY
(1915 ~ 1959)

Known as "Lady Day," she was called the greatest jazz vocalist of her time. Starting in 1933, she recorded with Benny Goodman, Teddy Wilson, and others. Notable songs include "Lover Man," "Strange Fruit." In this city, she often lived here.

PENNSYLVANIA HISTORICAL AND MUSEUM COMMISSION 1992

bar (BAR)—One of the vertical lines dividing a piece of music into equal units.

beat (BEET)—A recurring emphasis marking rhythm in music or poetry.

bebop (BEE-bop)—Bop; jazz characterized by complex harmonies, melodic lines, and constant shifting of accent and often played at very rapid tempos.

blues (BLOOZ)—Melancholy jazz melodies originating from African-American rhythms and lyrics.

boogie-woogie (BUH-gee-WUH-gee)—A beat-driven style of playing blues on the piano characterized by a steady rhythmic ground base of eight notes in quadruple time (four beats to each measure) and a series of off-the-cuff melodies made up without preparation or rehearsal.

chord (KORD)—A combination of notes sounded together in harmony.

fortissimo (for-TIS-ee-moh)—Very loud (in music).

harmonic (har-MON-ik)—An overtone (higher tone) of a primary note played on an instrument.

harmony (HAR-moh-nee)—A pleasant chord or progression of chords.

improvisation (im-proh-vih-ZAY-shun)—The act of improvising.

improvise (IM-proh-vihz)—To compose, recite, play, or sing without preparation (off the cuff).

jazz (JAZ)—Music of American origin characterized by improvisation, syncopation, and usually a regular or forceful rhythm.

key (KEE)—A system of related notes based on a particular note; the tone or pitch of a voice.

melody (MEL-oh-dee)—A sweet or agreeable arrangement or succession of sounds; a rhythmic succession of single tones organized as a pleasurable whole.

music (MYOO-zik)—Vocal, instrumental, or mechanical sounds having rhythm, melody, or harmony.

note (NOHT)—A tone; a written symbol used to indicate the duration and pitch of a tone by its shape and position on the staff.

obbligato (ob-lih-GAH-toh)—An important accompanying part in a musical composition.

pitch (PITCH)—The degree of highness or lowness of a musical note or a voice.

rhythm (RIH-thum)—An ordered, repetitive switching of strong and weak elements in the flow of sound; the pattern produced by the emphasis and duration of notes in music.

swing (SWING)—A kind of jazz that varies the time of the melody while keeping the accompaniment in strict time.

syncopation (sing-koh-PAY-shun)—A change to the accents in a passage of music caused typically by stressing the weak beat rather than the strong one (or vice versa).

tempo (TEM-poh)—The time, speed, or rhythm of a piece of music.

timbre (TIM-bur)—The characteristic quality of the sound produced by a particular voice or instrument; also spelled timber.

tone (TOHN)—A musical or vocal sound, especially with reference to its pitch, quality, and strength.

About the Author

Earle Rice Jr. is a former senior design engineer and technical writer in the aerospace, electronic-defense, and nuclear industries. He has devoted full time to his writing since 1993 and is the author of more than sixty published books. As the son of a professional jazz musician, he learned at an early age to savor and admire the unique and plaintively personal vocal renderings of the inimitable Billie Holiday. Earle is listed in *Who's Who in America* and is a member of the Society of Children's Book Writers and Illustrators, the League of World War I Aviation Historians, the Air Force Association, and the Disabled American Veterans.